SAYING GOODBYE

Andrew Stancek

Červená Barva Press
Somerville, Massachusetts

Červená Barva Press
P.O. Box 440357
W. Somerville, MA 02144-3222

www.cervenabarvapress.com

Bookstore: www.thelostbookshelf.com

Cover Art: "Prepostska Street" Courtesy Wikimedia Commons

Cover Design: William J. Kelle

ISBN: 978-1-950063-75-8

Library of Congress Control Number: 2023931063

ACKNOWLEDGMENTS

It has been a long, tortuous journey towards the birth of this book, with much rejection along the way, and I have only been able to persevere due to the support of a generous community.

In the earliest days I was able to carry on because of Gay Degani, Joani Reese, Susan Tepper, Matt Potter, Michelle Elvy, McKenna Donovan, Len Kuntz, Robert Vaughan, Stephanie Freele, Mary Akers, Avital Gad-Cykman, Barry Friesen, Richard Osgood, Tammy Sherwood.

Thanks to Christopher Allen, Randall Brown, Paul Beckman, April Bradley, Robin Stratton, Jen Knox, Stephen V. Ramey, Guilie Castillo, Steven Gowin, Jodi Paloni, Barry Basden, Jayne Martin, Cherise Wolas, John Riley, Meg Tuite, Jennifer Kircher, Gary Percesepe, Bill Lantry, Francine Witte, Caroline Couderc.

Much love to Ellen Parker, Patti Parkinson, Kim Chinquee.

Thanks to my workshop supporters Lee Martin and Cecile Callan.

Steve Almond and Jensen Beach.

I have benefitted from the workshop guidance and support of Kathy Fish and Meg Pokrass.

Special affection to my lifelong friends Blaine Adams, Russ Moore and only slightly later friends Pennie Bucilla and Karen Carlson.

I am beholden to Sara Lippmann and Nancy Stohlman for their generosity in providing positive comments on the book.

Gloria Mindock, publisher-extraordinaire, thank you, thank you.

I wish my mother, Jaroslava Blažková, were still here to help celebrate.

I appreciate the love and support of my children, Claire Marie Stancek and Matthew Stancek, and their spouses Daniel Benjamin and Joscelyn Owen Stancek.

Finally, absolutely none of it could have happened without the sharp editorial eye, careful attention to detail and loving support of my wife, Anne. Words cannot express my gratitude.

TABLE OF CONTENTS

In memory of Jaroslav Blažek, 20.7.1907 – 15.11.1971
and Helena Blažková, 20.9.1910 – 6.1.1970

For Anne, always

SAYING GOODBYE

Soldiering

Brave Soldier, that's my title.

Everyone has been calling me that for such a long time.

Once I had Dad. Then I didn't. Something happened and Mami did not talk about it and I did not talk about it. Nobody talked about it.

I used to have a space saved in my mind for Dad but once he disappeared, so did the space.

Then Mami stopped being there. When she reappeared, she didn't talk about where she'd been. I'd never know when she'd be there and when she wouldn't. Sometimes she was and sometimes she wasn't and I never knew.

She'd bring food, usually. We didn't talk about it. She'd come, with maybe three loaves of bread, three bottles of milk and a hunk of cheese and we ate. Another time a coil of sausage and a bunch of radishes. A bag of pastries. For two or three days I might not see her and I ate cheese, drank milk and didn't know if I should be saving food. I ate, not saving, usually.

One day she came home after I was asleep, woke me up, told me to brush my teeth and put on pajamas. She didn't say where she'd been, or how long she'd be home. I stared at the spidery wrinkle across her forehead and at her eyebrows and her neck. She yelled, "Don't look at me like that," and I hid under the kitchen table. She began to cry, took one plate after another from the credenza and threw them against the wall, yelling, "*Dost', dost', dost',*" which means "enough". She stopped and after a while I fell asleep under the table.

A few days later she came with a watermelon, cut it in slices and we each had three. She began pacing. She paced in the flat for three days, stopping occasionally to rock in a chair and mutter. Finally she stopped, called me a brave soldier and said I'll have a better place to live. I wanted to ask but didn't. I still had a space in my mind for her.

She said, "Pack the small blue suitcase with everything you want, everything you want to keep," and I did.

"Grandma and Grandpa love you and will look after you forever. It'll be better for you."

She was pulling her hair and biting her lip as she was saying that, peering back into the kitchen.

We took the streetcar to Grandma and Grandpa's. I knew she would just leave and she did.

In the Beginning

Mami pushed me through the doorway. Grandpa's cushy sweater with the patches on the elbows clutched and nuzzled me. Mami was already walking away. I turned my head and her steps were runs. She did not look back. I knew she didn't want to hear goodbyes. The door closed with a click.

I knew I'd live there for good and Grandpa knew, too. He hugged hard. I inhaled cherries sizzling -- Grandma was baking my favorite dessert – *bublanina*.

In my new kingdom I'd eat like a king, ride a shiny red bike, perform good deeds for my subjects. And I'd never think about Mami again.

Secrets and Escapes

The first month at Grandma and Grandpa's I spent rooting through the attic. Cobwebbed and sneezing, I brought treasures to Grandpa to hear their story.

"That magnifying glass, I remember -- must be, heavens, forty years since Captain Stodola used it to start a fire, saving us from frostbite. Later, a young recruit dropped it in the barracks. You and I will work on fire-starting our next sunny day."

"The cape with a rip, oh yes. Belonged to Kočkorád, the wizard. I apprenticed with him for a year, lifetimes ago. For his disappearing trick he'd wind the cape around himself, call on thunder, and be gone. As long as it was the end of the show, it worked but sometimes he disappeared too early and the audiences yelled and wanted to give our troupe a beating. You and I have not practiced enough magic for a disappearing trick. In a few years, maybe."

Grandpa and I did not talk about Mami who vanished, even without a cape. In the corner of the bedroom I shared with Grandpa, I had my own treasure horde, presents from Grandma: an officer's hat, a sailor's, an investigator's. Snuff, my stuffed mouse, I brought from my previous life and I whispered secrets to him nightly.

My days were busy but the night was always windy, shutters banged, owls hooted, tree branches crashed. Any day Mami might suddenly stand by my cot at midnight, shake my shoulder and say, "Wake up, we're running again." I was half-expecting a message, in Morse code perhaps, or for a stranger on the street to lean in and say, "Three o'clock tomorrow in front of the Manderlák." My rucksack with a ball of twine, a jackknife, a topographic map and a slingshot rested under my bed, next to my runners.

The day Mami came through the front door, calling "Hello, anyone home?" I hid behind Grandpa. He kissed both her cheeks, peered into her face and reached for the bottle of slivovitz.

"You're pale, too thin. Plum dumplings last night, your mom will bring a nice plate, with a shot or two on the side?"

Mami cringed. Her voice was hoarse, like she didn't use it anymore. She reached into her purse, brought out a matchbox sized package, paper torn in the corners.

"Your birthday present, Adam," handed it to me, staring at her shoes. "Hope you like it."

I peered at Grandpa, uncertain if I should open it. Grandpa patted her hand, touched her hair.

"We weren't expecting you today. You didn't come for…" he glanced at me. My sixth birthday, over a month ago, had ended with Grandma clearing the plate set aside, and she and Grandpa in a whisper-shouting fight about ingrates.

"So glad you came, Blanka."

She sat on the edge of her chair, hands white-clenched on the embroidered tablecloth. "Maybe Mom could come here," she said, "I want to, need to, talk to you both."

"Heli," Grandpa called, "come sit, visit with Blanka."

In the kitchen it sounded like three pots dropped, followed by another for emphasis.

Mami's face grew paler, her eye twitched. She twirled a strand of hair, stood up. "Maybe this is a bad idea."

"Damnation and thunderbolts, Heli, can you stop rumbling there and come?"

Grandma shuffled in, jaw set, wiping hands on a flowered apron, eyes ticking between the three of us, settling on her wedding picture on the mantel behind Grandpa.

"Adam, why don't you go outside to play?" Mami's voice was barely audible.

"Enough secrets," Grandma yelled. "Always whispers behind closed doors, special meetings, conspiracies. Nonsense. You have some new scheme or disaster to announce. Your son should hear it."

The vein on Grandpa's forehead throbbed purple; he cleared his throat to talk, but changed his mind. His look told me to stay put.

"I can't," Mami said. "I've tried but can't. It's hard on everyone and I wish I were stronger. I was going to send a postcard. But I've come to say goodbye. When I find a place, I'll let you know."

She shook like the rabbit when Grandma and I picked it out of the hutch to slit its throat for a roast. She squinted and I stared at the gouges on her jaw, the crack on the left lens of her glasses.

She took three steps to the door. "I'll…I'll write. Try not to hate me."

The door clicked behind her. I ripped the paper off the package she left: a miniature tow truck with whirring wheels. I snapped the winch off and shoved the truck into the coffee grounds in the garbage.

Rolling Out the Dough

I sat at the dining room table, my eyes didn't want to open and my tummy rumbled. The taste in my mouth was sour, not nice sour like a lemon drop but ugly sour like leaning over a toilet bowl; I concentrated on my breath going in and out.

All night long I'd dreamt of Mami dropping me off, of how she ran like a skittish cat as soon as she pushed me through Grandma and Grandpa's doorway, of how she went over on her ankle but kept stumbling, away, away, away. I was dreaming, swallowing snot but didn't want to wake Grandma. For a while Grandpa had his hand on my forehead and he whispered, "Sleep, Little One, sleep. You're safe."

The mug of something chocolatey in front of me was hot and a bowl of porridge steamed. My tummy jiggled and I ran to the bathroom. Porridge, no, I couldn't keep that down.

When I came out of the bathroom, Grandma was rolling dough in the kitchen. She didn't glance at me, kept the rolling pin going, sprayed a handful of flour on her surface.

"You don't have to eat if you don't feel like it this morning," she said. The kitchen smelled of sugar, cinnamon and vanilla; the pot on the stove was burbling soup stock. "In the drawer on the right," she said, "pull out a small apron, just the right size for an apprentice cook. You put it on and roll and then I'll show you how to form apricot dough balls."

I wanted to tell her about running, about Mami screaming, "Move, move. Faster." But I also only wanted to think about apricot dumplings with a poppyseed sauce and powdered sugar. It was toasty near the oven and I stood on a wooden stool with my own rolling pin and kept rolling.

Six Birthday Candles

You spend so long looking forward to a birthday, and when it arrives it's yelling, tears and slammed doors, and you wish never to have a birthday again.

Grandpa asked me what I wanted most, that six is a big boy, and I could ask for a big boy present. I said I wanted Mami and Dad to live with me again. As soon as the words came out, I knew I said the wrong thing, and Grandpa said his head was about to burst and he needed to go for a nap. That is a present I'm not getting.

Grandpa knows I want to become a bike racer, like Smolík, my hero, who won the Prague-Berlin-Warsaw road race, so I'm pretty sure I'm getting a bike, the second-best present. I'll learn to ride it racer-fast. I've learned to sleep on a fold-out cot. I've learned not to think about Mami and Dad. I can learn anything.

On the day of the birthday, I was eating my favorite soup, full of liver dumplings and Grandpa was smiling, blowing on his spoon, slurping, and Grandma was shuffling in with a platter of wiener schnitzels, her face red from working at the stove. A great occasion, all for me. Delicious food and yet my tummy told me they were pretending, that as soon as I was out of earshot, the fighting snakes would hiss again.

I finished my soup and Grandma sat down with us and we ate veal. Grandma is the best cook in the world. She won prizes for her baking before she was sixteen and she still has the certificates. But she wasn't even bothering to pretend she was happy. She ate a few bites, pushed the plate away and stared at Grandpa, who pretended not to notice. I wanted to keep eating the meat and potato salad, but Grandma was making my tummy squeak. I pushed my plate away, too.

"Well, let's see if there is a present for the man of the house," Grandpa said. "If you run to the lean-to, we'll meet you in a few minutes."

I ran. It was red, shiny and I kept ringing the bell. The sound bounced off the wall and I still heard, as they came up, Grandpa's mutter, "For the sake of the boy, try."

I walked the bike onto the road. The handlebars and the seat were high but as I stared at the brewery on the horizon, I felt my feet pedaling furiously away.

Infernal or Heavenly, Your Pick

Grandma stood in the doorway, left hand on a hip, lips quivering. A strand of hair had come down; she blew it out of her eyes; beads of sweat shimmered on her cheeks and her breath was ragged.

"You're waking the dead with the infernal banging and my head will burst and I can't take it anymore...," her voice broke and she started sobbing.

Grandpa turned the Blaupunkt radio down, way down. We were brass band marchers, he and I. My collection of assorted pot lids lined the floor and we banged, marching around the living room. At the important beats, I slammed my fist into the credenza door and the collection of liqueur glasses tinkled and Grandpa and I laughed: we were in Brass Band Heaven.

But we were in trouble now. Grandpa knew whatever he did would be wrong, that Grandma would wail and slam a door. The smell of cinnamon, baking apples and brown sugar wafted in from the kitchen. Grandma had put a dollop of whipped cream into my morning cocoa. But our infernal noises put us in the doghouse.

I sidled up to her, threw my arms around her big tummy, tugged on the apron splattered with tomato and beet stains.

"It was the music of heaven, Grandma," I said. "St. Peter was leading us in the marching. We're sorry we gave you a headache. If you lie down on the couch here, I'll get the Opoldekl ointment and massage your temples."

She patted the top of my head, tried to smile, put her ladle down.

"Cauliflower soup on the table in a few minutes. You marchers must be hungry after all your exercise."

Not Exactly Magic

The girl who moved into the house next to the Štetinas had pig-tails. Grandpa went over to introduce himself, welcome the family to the neighborhood and she flashed by as her mom was saying, "Your grandson looks about the same age as Yvette, maybe they'll be friends, play together." No other kids on our part of the street; I played with Maco who lived down the hill, but Grandma kept telling me she didn't want me going there anymore. What games could I play with a girl? She probably didn't like trucks and I wasn't going to play with dolls. She had a bike, and I was still learning mine, walking it, standing on the pedal as it rolled. I had a hard time getting my leg across without falling. My knees and elbows were pretty scraped. This Yvette, her bike looked pretty used.

Grandpa shook the hand of Mrs. Poliak, said, "Well, don't hesitate anytime you need anything, two houses over, my wife will be happy to see you."

Mrs. Poliak thanked him and I was glad they didn't say, "Go, play together." Grandpa and I walked to the store, picked up bread, cheese, milk, eggs, and he promised a new magic trick. We stopped along the path, watched a line of ants carrying white boulders to their anthill. "Building, always building," Grandpa said. "Never wonder why, or if they should be doing something else. They just are what they are." I almost said we all are what we are, but then I thought I often wonder about being somewhere else, maybe with Mami and Dad and I guess ants don't wonder like that. The sun was beating down and we were both sweating so we stopped the ant visit.

Grandma was cooking sauerbraten and dumplings; a cherry sponge cake was already out of the oven. The dumplings were also just what they were. In the garden of the Poliak house, three sunflowers, as tall as I, soaked up the sun. We hadn't had rain in a week and the ground was cracked. In the afternoon Grandma was sure to send me out to cut grass for the bunny. A sparrow pecked next to the parsley and the dill; the air was still.

Rooster Crowed

Grandma's strudel overflowed with cinnamon and cloves; her paper-thin apple slices were dipped in plum brandy. Visitors, demanding her recipe, always called it the best apple strudel in town.

She placed a large piece in front of me, with a dollop of whipped cream. But Grandpa's piece she slammed down and the fork bounced off the plate.

"You want me to be a widow," she said. "You never listen to me. Exercise and rest is what the doctor ordered. But do you take care of yourself?"

Grandpa grumbled. "Oh, Heli, you know I'm doing my best. The neighbors are so needy and the radios made so poorly. Once they've grown used to the broadcasts from Vienna and Berlin, to the concerts, to the football matches, they feel they can't live without. A little sunshine in their gardens is all they want. I can't say I'll get to it in three weeks, can I? I fix it in a few days, even if I sleep a little less and get up a little earlier. I'll try to stretch and lift and twist into those doctor contortions, I really will."

Back when Napoleon still guarded the house, whenever Grandma and Grandpa fought, he and I would crawl under the kitchen table and I'd curl into him and he'd wag his tail and lick my face. But ever since he was run over, I played under the table by myself.

When we strolled through our district, neighbors shook Grandpa's hand and patted his back. So what if he jiggled when he carried me piggyback? Mr. Kroner had a gut the size of a zeppelin and did no jumping jacks. For that matter, Grandma didn't go for jogs either. Then I remembered Grandpa last Easter, stretched out on the living room floor, jerking and turning blue, with Grandma screaming into the phone, "Send the ambulance. Hurry, for God's sake." If the doctor wanted him to exercise, he should. I would keep Grandpa company, lift barbells, build muscles next to him.

A fly struggled on the strip of fly paper by the window, wings flapping, recognizing its big mistake. Down the street the troops newly stationed in the barracks at Franconi performed their maneuvers. Two weeks of steady marching, right by our house. Grandpa said he sure felt safer now and Grandma gave him a look but didn't say anything.

Our rooster crowed outside. I loved to watch him parcel out corn to his favorite hens but I could not leave the house until I was sure Grandma and Grandpa made up. Grandma poured coffee into his huge mug and he made his eyebrows wiggle.

"Maybe the three of us can go for a walk this afternoon, gather linden blossoms for tea."

She nodded.

I tried to whistle through the gap between my front teeth but could only fizzle. Grandpa turned on his Blaupunkt radio, smiled at the final duet of The Bartered Bride. The hero tricks everyone, gets his bride as well as his inheritance.

Crossroads

I was lagging a dozen steps behind; Grandpa was whistling a csardas, reaching for the linden blossoms, placing them into Grandma's basket. The sun was baking my bare arms and the thistles were scratching my bare legs but I was whistling, too. I heard a hyena laugh, but Grandpa never stopped his concert so I was sure he didn't hear it -- probably just the wind. This morning, when I woke up, I saw Mami's coffin. I knew that was the last whisper of a nightmare. Nobody ever said Mami was dead. Thunder rumbles with no lightning.

Today the corners of Grandma's mouth were raised, her steps were lighter and not a grumble from her all day. We were inhaling the sweet smell; I could almost taste the linden tea. In the meadow ahead a few cows were lowing, huge bells around their necks. I picked thistle burrs, threw them at Grandma but my aim was off. The hum of Grandpa's voice near her ear was soft, the words butterfly wings.

At the edge of the fields they stopped, so I caught up. To the left the path towards the woods, rocky ground, squirrels, bird nests, mushrooms. To the right, down to the pond, a chance to splash, cool off. Or we could turn back. Grandpa raised his eyebrows, wanted me to make the call. I never wanted this day to end. Grandma wiped a bead of sweat off her forehead. Even after the leisurely stroll, she was out of breath. Grandpa liked to pretend he was my Golden-Antlered Deer, who can keep galloping for miles, but it was only two weeks since he'd been released from the hospital.

"A little rest on the grass and then to the pond?" I said. I saw splashes of color in the crown of a tree: indigo, orange, white. I trilled a deep-throated warble but the birds ignored me. Grandma's face was red and she rubbed her temples. Grandpa grimaced.

"We'll go splashing another time, Brave Knight. We'll take your Grandma home. I know strudel is awaiting us."

I cantered off; a breeze brushed my face. The tall grass swayed, a squeal, a thrash, a rust shadow ran. A bunny stared at me glass-eyed, insides spilt, the fox gone. The flies buzzed on the carcass already.

Six Rolls of the Dice

Lucky Seven: I woke up, a cold cloth across my forehead and the top of my pajamas soaking. Lights were blazing in the bedroom, Grandpa was clutching me and Grandma was muttering "Sweet Mother of Jesus, have mercy on us; Jezuskote we need an ambulance." The ache behind my eyes was splitting my head open and I remembered nothing. My throat was sore from screaming. I did not want to ask, did not want to know. Grandma held a mug of linden tea to my lips, so hot it burnt my tongue. I had a few sips and then we changed my clothes and turned out lights. I slept. In the morning they both peered at me, Grandpa drummed his fingers on his cheek, Grandma shivered.

Snake Eyes: When I waited for Grandpa by the streetcar station to come back from work, tons of women shuffled out. Ours is the first big stop on the outskirts of town and half the streetcar empties here. Sometimes a glimpse of a scarf, a hand sweeping hair off the forehead, or a clop of a heel made my heart think, "yes", but it never was. I never mentioned it to Grandpa and anyway I decided not to think about her, ever. So I didn't.

Four Legs on One and Me on the Other: The German Shepherd on the other side of the fence snarled, growled that if only he could find an opening in the fence, he'd rip me to pieces. I had a sword and a crown and flashed them at him but he laughed, bared his glinting teeth, "Let me through, and I'll show you who is King." Mr. Štetina, the neighbor, yelled for him to get inside, and told me I didn't need to be afraid, that Rex would only harm robbers. Maybe I am a robber, I thought, but I didn't tell him.

Three Kids and Still Just Me, Alone: The Bilak kids down the road were older, been living in their ramshackle house forever and Grandma told me to ignore them. They had thin-tired bikes, did wheelies in front of our house and made farting noises. I loved my red bike and knew I'd grow up to be a pro racer like Smolík, but I wasn't superfast yet. I rode too close to their house and when I turned back quickly, fell and scraped my knee. They laughed, called out, "Girlie Belly-Button." I rode back home like a typhoon and did not show them tears. Once I'm at the top of the podium I'll laugh.

Six and Two: Grandpa was carrying me in his arms. It didn't hurt too much but as blood was pouring down my calf I could see bone and my scream was loud enough to bring Grandpa. Grandma and Grandpa told me not to ride too close to the construction, to those sharp paving stones but to fly like Smolík you have to ride faster and faster. Grandpa said Doctor Foldvari in the mansion at the crest of the hill would stitch me up, that I am a brave soldier and will have many flesh wounds before I am kissing the girls. "Yecch," I said, "No girls, pleeeze."

Three of Us and One of Her: Grandma sent me out to gather gooseberries from the bush by the north fence. I was very fair: one for the bowl, one for my tummy. Two for the bowl, two for my tummy. Three for the bowl, three for my tummy. Some were tart and some were sweet. I liked the tart ones best. The red currants I spit out: too green. When Grandma baked, she let me lick the spoons. The kitchen smelled like heaven: dill and caraway and garlic and apricots. Mami's kitchen only smelled of empty cupboards and ants. I wondered if she had berries to eat, spoons to lick.

Run Towards

Through the brambles rush tearing the skin on my arms and legs I bolt can't fast enough too much brush underneath stumble pick myself up still no stop cannot stop never stop no no no have to have to have to keep going nothing else I am so hot so so hot water even a drop parched tongue keep going she is waiting waiting at the edge always been waiting should have started out earlier have to hurtle faster but I know now I know finally she is is yes I will see her I will be fine fine just fine then together yes always she will hold my hand won't ever leave ever and yes I know I can get there

Snatches

The crone was hunched, humming a tuneless melody and she jerked the second she saw us approaching.

Before we'd set out, Grandma squeezed my hand hard and said to remain close to her throughout the whole market trip, to not get distracted by a colorful parrot, an odd fruit or a sweet-smelling treat, to stay right by her and to scream like a puppy with a leg under a truck if anyone laid a hand on me.

"Not a fairytale place," she warned, "children get snatched, never seen again."

Night after night Grandpa told me tales of princes rescuing maidens, of brave boys saving kingdoms, of soldiers on blood-curdling missions, and mostly he concluded with a "happily ever after." But now Grandma wanted to frighten me.

"I'm brave, Grandma," I said. "If anyone tried to snatch me, I'd lop off their arm with my sword, turn them into stone with a spell."

Grandma squinted, another warning on the tip of her tongue. "Just stay close. I want you to know where your food comes from. But it's crowded."

We'd already picked up potatoes, beets, a bagful of fresh sauerkraut when we saw the crooning dark woman. She cut her song-whine short, stared at me, wiggled a small finger. "Come, boy. We've been waiting. What took you so long? So many messages from your mother. It's time. Now."

My heart beat like a scared bunny's. I took a step towards the woman and Grandma yanked me back.

"Hush!" she yelled at the woman. "Stop your jabbering. You know no one, know nothing." She grabbed my hand, dragged me by the barrels of pickles, by the stands of live chickens tethered by their legs to tent poles, by the mounds of crushed ice with carp sides on top, by whole fish staring with blank eyes.

"Grandma," I cried. "Mami sent a message. She wants to see me."

"Tripe. Offal. Gypsy trickery. They know all the boys are longing for their mothers, know what line of gibberish to spout. She knows nothing about your mother. We'll get a policeman to put fear into her."

I looked back. Already the spot where the woman had her blanket with soft cheeses and wood carvings was empty; she was nothing but vapor.

"But Grandma, Mami might have."

Grandma stopped our march in front of a sausage vendor. She shoved a long Parisian wurst into my hand. "Mustard on the little table," she pointed. "Eat. Stop imagining castles."

I took a bite. I knew I'd be back.

Shards

Always shards and always weather.

Mami, back when, would yip and throw whatever was closest: a wine glass, a vase, a hat, a pencil sharpener. Then waves of louder screeching, then ebbing, and then the storm would peter out. We had to pretend it never happened; the shards would disappear and a new vase sprout in the old spot. But at night, going to the bathroom, I would tread softly to make sure I didn't step on broken glass. Each storm different but also the same. I scurried to make sure I wasn't in hitting range, disappeared under a table and listened and watched from a safe spot until the typhoon passed. Dad, the center of it, normally laughed and shrugged. One time, though, he thundered back, hoarse and purple-faced and when his explosion ended, he slammed the door so hard that a flower pot crashed in the hallway and the dragon knocker echoed on the outside door. I crawled into bed, blankets over my head, and waited for my teeth to stop chattering.

So now it wasn't dawn yet and I had daytime clothes on, fifteen crowns in my pocket, ready to run, but the door creaked when it wasn't supposed to and then I bumped into the credenza. Grandpa stood in the bedroom doorway and whispered, "What on earth?" and I could not run after all.

"Back to the market," I said. "They'll take me to Mami and she'll want me. I know which streetcar to take, I do."

His shaking hand pointed. "Into the kitchen. Let's not wake your Grandma at this ungodly hour."

We sat across from each other and Grandpa stared at me. His forehead was creased, his left hand was rat-tat-tatting and his eyes were flashing lightning bolts. I wanted to be fog and then nothing.

"It's a trick," he finally pushed out through his teeth. "Your mother is not sending any messages. She does not live in this part of the country. She does not want to see you. She's gone."

My body shook. "That's not true...the woman said...she has messages...Mami's waiting."

Grandpa continued to frown but his expression grew less stormy.

"We should have talked more. I'm sorry. But you cannot rush off on your own, cannot put yourself in danger."

I did not cry when she said she's leaving, that she'd leave me at Grandma and Grandpa's. Now I could not stop.

"Let's get you changed back into your jammies, get a little sleep. We'll talk soon, I promise."

I didn't want to. I knew I couldn't possibly sleep. But somehow my eyes closed.

Bravery

Bravery comes in all sizes and sometimes a corn-sized kernel is awfully big.

I am a big boy but sometimes I don't feel like it. I have a sword and a suit of armor. I have a blanket for courage during the night. My heart is full but sometimes it quakes and forgets how to be brave. I know it's OK to cry. Mami has cried and Grandma has cried and even Grandpa has cried, and Grandpa, I know, is the bravest of all. But you don't want to be a crybaby, that's for sure.

When Grandpa found me in the hallway, ready to run, and when he was thundering at me, I was both sad and brave; I had to do what I had to do. He said Mami doesn't live in town, doesn't send messages, doesn't want me. Grandpa tells the truth, but he might not know. I still think of the market. He says that is nothing but trouble. I'm not sure what to do, but I think I do.

Once upon a time Grandpa was someone I'd visit for a few days and he'd perform magic tricks and tell jokes and whistle. That Grandpa is gone, just like Mami and Dad are gone. He sits next to me and they don't, but still that Grandpa is gone. I love him the same way but everything is different. When the bucket on my excavator broke off, Grandpa used a soldering iron to reattach it and it looked the same, but wasn't. Sometimes I want everything to be the way it was a long time ago but then I remember the screams, running and hiding and I don't. I have to listen to Grandpa and obey him. But he's not the Golden-Antlered Deer anymore.

Treasures, Treasures Everywhere

Mr. Znojmo, who ran the grocery store, had a gold tooth. When he laughed, he threw his head back, mouth wide open, and at the back of his mouth, I clearly saw a glint of gold. First time, I thought I imagined it, but he laughed frequently, asked the women with downturned mouths about their rheumatism and ailing husbands, checked with pretty Vierka that her new fiancé was treating her like a queen, handed me a *kifli* to chew while we waited in line -- everyone received a joke and a smile. I kept staring and sure enough, gold at the back of his mouth.

"Mr. Znojmo, did you put a gold treasure into your mouth, so no one can steal it?"

Grandma turned red and dropped the yellow onion she was holding. It rolled under the pastry shelves but I didn't crawl under to fish it out. I was waiting for his answer.

"So sorry, Mr. Znojmo," she stuttered, "the boy does not know to hold his tongue."

But Mr. Znojmo was laughing. "The boy has a good eye and an inquisitive mind. I like that in a young man. And treasure? Why, the fruits and vegetables, the fresh pastries, the smelly cheeses and juicy cold meats, that's the only treasures around here. In my mouth, little soldier, that's only a thin covering to protect the tooth, like the cloths we put over the pears and plums overnight, to keep them from soaking up too much humidity. My little bit of gold shines and sparkles, like Vierka's smile, but is no treasure at all."

Grandma laughed, Vierka tittered but I kept my eyes on him. Maybe he didn't want to admit to a gold horde in his mouth. Maybe he had others as well. In his ears? Around his neck, on that chain he wore?

Mr. Znojmo rang up a few customers' groceries, then turned back to us.

"As I was saying, this is clearly an exceptional young man. I could use a pair of hands at our busy times, bagging groceries, stocking shelves, filling up the pastry bins. Do you think you'd like to help in exchange for some treats and a little food to take home?"

I looked up at Grandma; she frowned.

"He's awfully young, Mr. Znojmo; he'd only be in the way here."

I loved treats, loved helping. Maybe I'd find other treasures. The store had many doors, a walk-in fridge which puffed out icy clouds, ovens in the back.

"Grandma, I won't get in the way. Can I, please, please?"

He was laughing again, the gold tooth glinting.

"An adventure," he said. "You can start tomorrow."

Grumbles

Chicken soup was simmering and Grandma was peeling potatoes, muttering.

"Absolute nonsense. Much too young. Something else to worry about. How do I know he'll be safe?"

She wasn't talking to me or Grandpa. Whoever happened to respond would be scorched to a crisp like bread in a defective toaster. I was playing with my dump truck, a little mouse. Grandpa was lying down on the couch in the living room, half-listening to Beethoven and half-sleeping. Another half might have been listening to Grandma, but he knew better than to say anything. The whole house was simmering.

Mr. Znojmo offered, Grandma snorted, but when we came home and she presented the idea to Grandpa, he thought it terrific, and I turned cartwheels. She said she wouldn't walk me there, but when Grandpa said, "I'll take him then," she yelled, "Absolutely not," and slammed the door.

When I skipped into the store, Mr. Znojmo was bringing out a crate of pears, Alenka was slicing salami at the deli counter and three women lined up at the cash register. Mr. Znojmo put his crate down, then his face lit up.

"Goodness, I forgot all about my little helper. Busy day, give me a sec and I'll get you started."

Grandma squeezed my hand, blew her nose loudly. Mr. Znojmo bustled back.

"So, Little Soldier, reporting for duty? Ready to march, one-two-three?" He laughed and I again saw the gold in his mouth. I nodded. He turned to Grandma.

"Two hours, we agreed? He'll earn his keep, maybe with a bite or two from the deli? All set?"

No smile in Grandma's eyes.

"You be good," she said, kissed the top of my head. "I'll be back."

Mr. Znojmo handed me an apron. "We'll start you on apples."

Gooseberry Pie

Laundry day, an ordeal of strains and sweats, with Grandma's face growing redder and redder. She sent me to gather gooseberries, not be underfoot, told me to grab a bun when I was ready for lunch, spread jam on it on my own, like a big boy.

The laundry room was in the basement, where no one ever went except to scrounge for potatoes or a spare part in storage. She had a huge washtub and a metal board with ridges, brushes with hard bristles, a mangle with a hand crank and a vat of reeking starch.

I sprawled on the ground outside to watch through a little window and breathed in billowing clouds of steam and lye. I made sure I didn't cough or sneeze, so she wouldn't know I was spying. She wore her old polka dot dress, rolled the sleeves up to her shoulders, scrubbed the sheets over the board with the brushes. Even outside where I was, the steam clouds made me gag. The other night Grandpa said he'd buy one of the new-fangled washing machines we saw in the window of the appliance store on Štúrova Street, but Grandma shook her head and said no point in wasting hard-earned money on nonsense like that, when for hundreds of years women washed their clothes the good old-fashioned way. Grandpa opened his mouth a couple of times like a carp in a wooden barrel at the market, no words and as usual, he gave up.

Grandma scrubbed and scrubbed and I gave up watching. She was out of breath, peony red, working in stops and starts. I took my bowl and skipped to the corner of the yard to visit the gooseberry bushes, weighed down with heavy golden berries. I squeezed one to feel and smell the pulp on my fingers -- sour-delicious. I popped three in my mouth. Grandma made pie out of them but I liked them best right off the bush. I picked a few for the bowl and when a dragon-fly hovered by, I followed. He led me to the grave where we buried old Micinka, after she stopped her wheezing. Her fur was patchy and one eye closed after she was beaten up by the Steiner's tom. I was sure she didn't care for gooseberries but I picked three dandelions, put them on her grave. No more berry-picking.

Hunger

Grandpa shook his head, his usually soft eyes frosty.

"You don't know hunger. You know a slight discomfort, a little twinge telling you that a treat might be nice. Hunger is a cramp when for three days all you'd had is melted snow and a third of a shriveled pippin. Hunger is your little sister giving up her wail in the wicker basket. Hunger is chewing on tree bark and leaves you'd dug out from under the snow. Hunger —" He slapped his hand on the table.

"Enough." His hands shook and a vein throbbed in his forehead. His breaths were short as he stared out the window at the pear tree.

"I don't know why I'm going on like this. You and I will have some eggs and cake and I'll tell you about heroic deer and brave princes, about marzipan and Turkish delight. Mustn't let reality attack."

I wanted to cry but clenched my teeth. I should have held my tongue, not whined. Since Grandma was admitted to the hospital, everything was topsy-turvy and when I went to pee in the night, the light was still on and Grandpa was snoring in the rocking-chair. I walked over to the mantel, picked up the photograph of Mami and Dad smiling at each other on their wedding day. It was a sunny day in the picture. I spit on my forefinger and wiped off a smudge.

Dust to Dust

Grandma was dead, Grandpa was sobbing, and Mami was still gone.

Grandpa's whole body was shaking. I said, "There, there," just like he had when I let the rabbit out of the hutch and the neighbor's cat swatted him and Puňťo squealed and twitched and was dead. But Grandpa was heaving like he would vomit and couldn't stop.

Grandpa always knew what to do. Grandma knew cakes and dumplings and parrot cages. Grandpa knew straight spine and saying the right words and especially not speaking. When Mami and I appeared at the doorstep and I rang the bell, it was Grandpa who opened the door and Mami pushed me forward. I looked at him, not her, and something happened in his eyes. His chin trembled, he pulled me in and did not call out after her.

He'd been in hospital, and the doctor said for him to exercise and Grandma grumbled he wasn't taking good enough care of himself, but we knew he'd be there for us forever. We did not know about Grandma, just like we hadn't known about Mami.

The kitchen smelled of garlic and fried caraway, burnt cinnamon and brown sugar from the *buchty* Grandma baked two days ago. My tummy gurgled. I shouldn't be thinking of sweets at a time like this but my tummy didn't know to behave. I squished an ant with my thumb, made him into mush.

Everybody was always leaving in this house. I knew I would live here forever, not leave.

"Liverwurst in the fridge, pumpernickel in the breadbox," Grandpa said.

Rain and Shadows

We met the rain.

I stuck out my tongue and felt the cold of the drops. Grandma was in the drop spreading over my tongue. She grumbled; I heard her rasp. She did not think Grandpa was dressed warmly enough, that he'd catch his death of cold, told me to look after him better. I laughed. Glad to be with you again, Grandma, I told her.

I wanted the rain to wash away the memory of her face in the coffin, the dark wine stain under her eye which the undertaker only made paler with his powder.

We continued to trundle along, rain or no rain. Cowbells in the distance. Did they keep them out at night? Perhaps the cows had sheds, little roofs to hide under, perhaps their hides were thick enough they didn't mind rain. My hide was not thick enough. I felt rain inside my underwear. I stumbled over a rock and Grandpa steadied me. I wanted to tell him I felt Grandma but thought he must feel her all the time, in his bones.

I stuck out my tongue again, to get another helping.

Bruno

"Bruno was the shaggiest dog anyone in the village had ever seen, so shaggy that his fur dragged in the puddles. When he shook, he splashed mud over everyone and some people laughed and some cursed. My brothers and I would take him down to the creek to wash him, good for an hour or two."

Grandpa's voice was shaking. He made us *lecso* for dinner and I told him it was delicious although it was nothing like Grandma's. Neither one of us mentioned her; Grandpa watched the foam on his beer go down and wiggled his foam mustache but I didn't laugh. Sometimes we laughed remembering an adventure, but a lot of the time he sighed and I went to the bathroom to cry.

My tummy was rumbling from the peppers and the paprika. Recently a lot of Grandpa's stories had been about his brothers, about their growing up together. He missed his brothers, as well as Grandma and I wanted to console him. I'd been going to the Štetinas' house and the Ďurinkas' house to play with their dogs. We couldn't get a dog: too much trouble. But I knew why he was reading me a Bruno story.

The Beasts Are Gone

Grandpa sneezed, a joke about to be made, and sneezed again. He held a cloth handkerchief to his nose and sneezed one more time. He shook his head, swallowed hard. Every house in the neighborhood had colds but we had been spared so far, have continued our explorations of the country. Last week we took a train trip to Žilina, walked the cobblestoned streets in the center of town, visited the local history museum and in spite of the cold air, had an ice cream cone.

"Because there is nobody around to tell us we can't," he laughed. "We don't have to show common sense." When I dripped a blob onto a newly pressed shirt he shrugged. Grandma was not here to scold.

Was he coming down with something? A cold? Something worse? Was it the fault of the ice cream? Grandpa once talked at me about viruses but I hadn't paid attention.

Women from the neighborhood kept dropping in, sometimes twice a week, sometimes four times, with a stew or a soup pot. Yesterday it was Mrs. Filipovská who shook her head and said, "The boy cannot stay here with you. Time to make decisions." Grandpa hustled them out lickety-split but some didn't take the hint. Mrs. Voříbková, a widow for five years, had three cherry trees in her yard and used to enter baking competitions, tried to make jokes when she came. She trailed a cloud of perfume and had a rainbow on her eyelids. She didn't get all fineried up when she hurried to the grocery store, I knew that. Grandpa rolled his eyes when I asked him about her.

"She needs no whetstone for her tongue," he said. "I'm too old to get bossed around, even if she won the Strudel Olympiad."

"I think I'd better lie down for a while," he said, "snuggle into an extra blanket for a nap. When I get up, we'll have a little linden tea and one of the pastries that what's-her-name brought. You can read our book; read it out aloud to me later."

I do the voices almost as well as he does. But when he shuffled off to the bedroom he was hunched and dragged his feet.

The Name of the Tree

I was sitting back in the corner seat of the milk-run train to Banská Bystrica. We missed the express: I had had too much tea at breakfast, and had to keep lining up at the train station where the bathroom stank of pee, beer and vomit. The bathroom-keeper granny kept repeating, "It's fifty halers, or a crown if you need toilet paper," Grandpa was waiting for me outside the washroom; I knew he was anxious about missing the train but I could not do anything about it. Finally, when I came out, the crackly public address system was announcing the very last call for the Banská Bystrica express, all the way down on platform 12. I shook my head and so did he, and he lined up to change our tickets from the express to the slow train.

I was pretty tired. Mami haunted me again in my dreams, the whispered words crinkling and I could not make out a single one. She wanted me to do something and I cried, "I don't understand." She slashed her arm like she was throwing an ashtray and disappeared into a fog. When I woke up, I was sweaty and my head hurt.

I closed my eyes. I didn't want to fall asleep, just in case she came back, but then if she did come back, maybe the air would be pink and cloud-balloony and we'd plan a trip to the beach to splash in the water. I fell asleep and heard froggy voices announcing the names of the stops every few minutes but the croaks burbled through a glass of water and I felt a blanket over my knees which Grandpa must have brought with him and when I woke up, he smiled and said, "Only two more hours".

We read our tree book together and sometimes when I looked out the window, we passed trees and I said, "That's a linden," and "That's a willow," and "That's a poplar," and he knew I was only making a joke and said, "You are a regular forester now, maybe we'll find a rare species in the forest, and become famous."

At the next stop he leaned out the window and bought two wursts from the vendor and a raspberry soda. We munched and I refused to think of anything sad.

Robbers

The train had a dining car, where Grandpa promised we could order ham and eggs with ketchup, bratwurst with sauerkraut or beef soup. Grandpa did not even ask if I was hungry; he knew. We stored luggage in our compartment, I placed the book about insects on my seat and Grandpa spread out the Italian sports car manual on his, and we went to enjoy.

Only one waiter was serving the whole car and almost all the tables were taken. As we went by the waiter, Grandpa slid him a fifty crown note and said, "I'll have a large Urquell and the boy a raspberry soda. We'll be sitting over there and when you serve us the drinks, we'll order food," and the waiter nodded. I always wanted a sausage, always, so that's what I asked for; Grandpa rubbed his hands about the stew and another beer. We watched the world whizzing by, cows grazing in the fields, funny-shingled houses and mutts running everywhere. Grandpa sighed, but he smiled at me, too.

"We have much to be thankful for, Sprite, don't we?" he said. I didn't mention Grandma although I knew he was thinking about her. If it weren't for her dying we wouldn't be having this trip, so something good always grows out of something awful, like mushrooms out of manure.

The sausage was yummy, the mustard sweet-sharp and Grandpa said he'd teach me a magic trick once we were settled in the mountains. One field we passed pastured a herd of goats and the one next to it was all sheep. The town where we'd be staying, Terchová, was the home of Juraj Jánošík, the Slovak Robin Hood, who robbed the rich and handed out bags of gold coins to the poor. His enormous statue stood on the edge of town. In the museum, they let you touch his boots and admire his axe and hat. If I don't become a bike racer, I think I'll be a robber.

Betrayal

Grandpa and I were travelling into the Tatra Mountains, armed with sleeping bags, hiking boots, hats, gloves, compass, even a bowie knife.

Grandpa interrupted our nightly reading of Scheherazade with a war novel starring local real-life heroes, Gabčík and Kubiš, who assassinated Reinhard Heydrich, the monster who thought up The Final Solution. Grandpa's voice shook as he read about them because of his personal connection to the story: he knew someone who was at school with Kubiš.

In the novel, the heroes are given cyanide pills to secrete inside their mouths. If the mission had to be aborted, or they were about to be captured, they'd bite down on the cyanide. No one could resist German torture, so anyone with valuable information promised to kill himself rather than betray comrades.

Grandpa's voice broke the first time the word "betray" appeared. The word shook me, too, made me wonder if I've been betrayed, first by my parents, and then by Grandma, if I'd been abandoned. But then I looked up at Grandpa's warm eyes, remembered his arms around me.

In a war, I would lead a mission with thousands of lives at stake. After succeeding, I wouldn't betray anyone. In the face of the enemy, I would laugh and bite hard.

Screaming

I was dreaming of a hunt. Three German Shepherds were running through corn field stubble and more dogs were snarling ahead and behind me men with shotguns and heavy boots stomped. I was trying to remember what we were hunting and one of the dogs peered at me, teeth gleaming. Suddenly I realized I was the one being hunted, and any second they'd realize it, too. A rasping voice called my name and I struggled to make out where it was coming from and I woke.

It wasn't a cry anymore, only a gasp. I ran, saw Grandpa on the floor, his face red, eyes fluttering. I screamed but didn't stop. I knew the drill. In his bedside table he had the vial of nitroglycerin. Two under the tongue. I found the vial, my hands shook and heart raced, I had three in my fingers, dropped one but stuck the two under his tongue. He was breathing; I saw and heard his breath. I wanted to remain by him, cover him, coo to him, but his life depended on my speed. The Štetinas next door had a phone; we didn't.

It was a whirr. I didn't know whom I talked to, how I managed to plead for help. My breaths all said, "He's OK, he's OK, he's OK."

He was lying on his back in an ambulance, oxygen mask on; I was strapped to a seat near him. I remembered clutching his arm when they tried to put him on the gurney and a paramedic saying, "Let go, let go now, you can come, too." He was breathing. I heard his breath. I heard my breath. The ambulance had the Vienna Autofahrer Auf dem Weg radio broadcast on, which Grandpa and I listened to Saturday afternoons. I recognized Beethoven, a sonata Grandpa and I often conducted. He was not conducting now. The ambulance was zipping along the wet road superfast, much faster than any streetcar. Almost no traffic, dark. I kept breathing, in-out, in-out. His eyes were closed. The driver and paramedic next to him were talking softly.

"And then she said," one chuckled and I realized for them this was another normal day.

Thunder and Lightning

Once the ambulance stopped, the world sped up, all the attention on Grandpa. I stumbled to the side. A nurse noticed me after a while, put both her hands on my shoulders, moved her face into mine.

"Terrible for you. But only doctors and nurses can be with him now. They'll examine him behind these doors, and do their very best, so he can go back home with you. You sit in this corner right here and wait. When they know something, they'll come tell you. I'll have a peek at you every now and then. Deal?"

I nodded. She smelled like strawberries and her eyes were deep blue wells.

"Would you like a chocolate milk and a sugared *šiška?*"

I was always hungry. I didn't remember when I last ate.

"My boy, Martin, is about your age," she said. "I have a coloring book ready for when he's waiting for me, with some crayons. You can color while you wait."

I never cried in the ambulance but her kindness made me swallow hard. I didn't usually do coloring, preferred a book to read, but I didn't bring one, and didn't want to ask her. Coloring might be fine for a time like this. My jacket was wet. Must have been raining when they put him into the ambulance.

Flood

For three nights when I went to bed it was raining and when I went to the bathroom in the night it was raining and when I got up it was raining. Grandpa and I used to love the illustrated book of Bible stories. Noah is the best story. Noah works hard and obeys when no one else does, and everyone laughs at him when he builds a boat, unlike any other boat. Grandpa said one of the lessons is never to give up even when no one else believes. When I first came to live with Grandma and Grandpa, I was scared and had my clothes, jackknife and sling in a rucksack under the bed, waiting for Mami to come sweep me up in the middle of the night, or a hoarse-chuckling man to come take me away. Grandpa often sat at the side of my bed. But I don't keep a rucksack there any more, even now with Grandma dead and Grandpa in the hospital.

Mr. Štetina took me to his house to sleep while Grandpa was in the hospital, set up a bed for me in a tiny room next to the kitchen, and they always have a little fire going in the stove. Mrs. Štetinová baked a plum upside-down cake and put a dollop of whipped cream on top of my morning cocoa. They smile at me slowly in the morning and I agreed that it would be too scary to be in Grandpa's house all by myself during the night.

When I visit Grandpa in the hospital, he whispers softly, in between his naps. I think his voice doesn't work all the way yet. Mr. Štetina had the radio on in the car when he took me to the hospital, and the announcer sounded worried this morning, saying the Danube was ready to spill, that the army is coming to build barricades out of sand bags; it is still rising and there is no end to the rain. Grandpa and I used to watch the big boats on the Danube. I remember one that had cranes and bulldozers and cement mixers but Grandpa said Noah's boat would have been a lot bigger, to have room for all the animals. We didn't laugh when we saw it and no one is laughing now about the pounding rain.

I told Grandpa it's a good thing I have my red ribbon in swimming, that I can swim fifty meters and not get out of breath. His eyes drooped and he fell asleep again. I have to believe the army will stop the water, that the rain will stop, that Grandpa will get strong enough to come home.

Spiral

"Mami," I called out when I woke in the middle of the night and I didn't know where I was, but as soon as the word left my lips, I knew that was wrong and I was embarrassed. I said I wouldn't think about her anymore, and now, suddenly, because of a stupid dream, I was thinking about her. I chased that picture away.

Then I remembered the gypsy at the market, what she said, and maybe it was real, even if Grandpa said it wasn't. He thought she is in a different part of the world, thinking about her own things, not me things. But even if when she was leaving, if she thought that was all there was, maybe she changed her mind, No. No. I won't think like this.

I turned on my bedside lamp. I was in a strange room but I remembered why I was here. Grandpa was sick. He was in the hospital. Grandma, oh, I remembered. And because there was no one left in Grandma and Grandpa's house, the Štetinas suggested I sleep in their house for a while. What if…No. They have given me a place to be. Grandpa was recovering in the hospital. I would see him later today. Mr. Štetina had given me a cuddly to sleep with, from a box in their attic, one that used to be their son Michal's once upon a time. It was furry and only had one eye and the tail was half hanging on. It was a cat-dog-clown and I thought I'd call him Balík. That's a good name, strong and manly. He smiled at me and I hugged him. He had been loved lots, I could tell, and he was happy to be out of the attic and back on a bed. I'll tell him what I'm thinking when I can't tell Grandpa. But Grandpa will be fine. I turned out the light again. I pulled a blanket close to my chin and hugged Balík.

"Good night, Little One," I said.

Sunset

Grandpa was sleeping. Again. He was pretty well sleeping all the time but at least I saw his chest moving. The machines he was hooked up to beeped and tapped and the monitors blinked. I sat by his bedside and breathed with him.

The day we came, yesterday, three days ago, a week ago? I don't know, was the worst. I sat in the corner, not sure about anything, I just knew he couldn't die, couldn't leave me, that he wouldn't. After a while Mr. Štetina came by, sat with me. He knew what happened because we used his phone to call the ambulance. He smelled of cough drops and cherry pipe tobacco, always wore a wine-colored baggy sweater. He really liked Grandpa. Sometimes he came over and they listened to Beethoven together while I played with trucks. He might visit for two hours and after saying, "Good day" they only sat and listened, but when he left, he always said, "So nice talking to you." I used to think it funny, but don't anymore. You can talk even if nothing is coming out of your lips. When I sat next to sleeping Grandpa now, I talked to him, too.

Doctor Hlavatý spoke to me this morning, didn't treat me like a baby. He said it was a heart attack, but not too bad a one, and that Grandpa is in pretty good shape for his age, and he should be OK, will have to exercise and not do too much, not overeat. I laughed and said that's exactly what Grandma used to say.

"Then," I said and my tears started flowing, "she died. She's not feeding us too much anymore. No *bublanina*, no dumpling with dill sauce. We don't overeat now."

The doctor patted my hand. "You're a brave soldier. Sure wish I could talk to one of your parents."

The files must have told him Mami can't be found, that we haven't seen Dad in forever. Mr. Štetina brings me in, goes downtown for his errands, picks me up again. I wanted Grandpa to be back home soon.

SAYING GOODBYE

I walked through the hospital halls, looked out the window. There was a soccer field on one side, a row of birches. Someone left a comfortable chair next to the window and yesterday I sat and watched a blood red sunset. The birches swayed in the wind and waved goodbye.

Snowflakes

The snow began as a few stray flakes, lonely and lost, before landing on the trees and the garden and sidewalk. Then a loud wind whooshed in and the sky grew dark and the flakes became stronger, strident, thousands of companions all coming down together, like a troop of soldiers, gathering into piles.

Grandpa has been released from hospital and I look after him. He is very tired, his voice is pale and his smile is like a wisp. We listen to Beethoven, muted, in the background. We don't talk much.

Mr. Štetina has helped to arrange whatever we can and the three of us have sat together to talk. For now Grandpa can be at home. The doctor at the hospital said it would be better if he convalesced for a month or six weeks in a sanatorium, but we thought it would be better still if we were together in his own home, if people helped. So for four hours a day Mrs. Bartlíková will come to clean and cook and fluff up his pillows, and then at night for two hours a nursing assistant will come to put him to bed, give him nighttime medications. Neighbors have been bringing pots of goulash and cakes and pastries, patting my head, calling me brave.

No news about Mami or Dad or anyone else. The gypsy hooting about Mami wanting me must have been a trick. Mr. Štetina told me he tried everything to contact her, and he's found no trace. She doesn't want to be found, as Grandpa said.

I'm scared sometimes. But I know I can. Grandpa was shaking, when the woman from Social Services said the best place for me would be the orphanage, that all the children get used to it quickly. Grandpa's breath was shallow, and he lifted his head up and roared, "No. Not happening. Absolutely out of the question." She frowned, scribbled on her pad, and left soon after. She didn't think I should be hearing them talk in the first place, but Grandpa insisted.

Grandpa had talks with neighbors he's known for years and two families said they'd take me in, treat me as a member of the family, give me a home. I want to stay with Grandpa but that cannot be forever. I know that now. In a few days it'll be my birthday. The families who might be my new family are coming. Cake and sparklers and snow and a new life. Right now, the snow is hurtling around. I see faces in the whirlwind.

ABOUT THE AUTHOR

Andrew Stancek describes his vocation as dreaming – clutching onto hope, even in turbulent times. He has been published widely, in *SmokeLong Quarterly*, *FRIGG*, *Hobart*, *Green Mountains Review*, *New World Writing*, *New Flash Fiction Review*, *Jellyfish Review*, *Peacock Journal* and *The Phare*, among others. Among his contest wins are the London Independent Story Prize, the Reflex Fiction contest, and the New Rivers Press American Fiction contest. His work has appeared in Best Microfiction 2021, the Bending Genres Anthology and Bath Flash Fiction anthologies. He has been nominated for the Pushcart Prize.

www.ingramcontent.com/pod-product-compliance
Lightning Source LLC
Chambersburg PA
CBHW030530260626
47157CB00005B/1960